Mars Trailor

Harini

pencil

ISBN 978-93-5667-504-9
© Harini 2023
Published in India 2023 by Pencil

A brand of
One Point Six Technologies Pvt. Ltd.
123, Building J2, Shram Seva Premises,
Wadala Truck Terminal, Wadala (E)
Mumbai 400037, Maharashtra, INDIA
E connect@thepencilapp.com
W www.thepencilapp.com

DISCLAIMER: *This is a work of fiction. Names, characters, places, events and incidents are the products of the author's imagination. The opinions expressed in this book do not seek to reflect the views of the Publisher.*

Author biography

Seeing a 10 year old so invested in writing books is a rare sight . From the second she could think, Harini made up thousands of stories in her own head. From tales about dragons to a Mystery novel. She would spin tales out of any idea she got. While writing *Mars Trailor*she made three different stories revolving around Mars, and chose the best version.

CONTENTS

Epigraph

As 18 year old Mars Trailor, gets exiled from the nation of I'Lexio... She is given hope by the arrival of a letter addresed to her by an unknown person, requesting her to buy a strange liquid. Which turns out to save her life. the next day she has returned to I'Lexio but never expects a war that died away a decade ago would re-ignite after her arrival.

Prolouge

*A **ruin** now stood, where the **white festival** was held...*

*All the **decorations, lights, entertainment, food** and **the entrance** itself were all turned to **ash**...*

*She didn't know where to go now, but an **unfamiliar** hand put itself on her shoulder.*

*'Let's go to **I'Lexio**, shall we...**Mars**?'*

Exile

Chapter One

-Exile-

Mars Trailor was not only a pheonix but a citizen of the I'Lexio nation. She had almost all of the human features and characters. She had short black hair and eyes that were as gold as a crown.

But even with her seemingly human traits, she was anything but a human to the world. She had a dark purple halo, and black wings. And these two traits had ruined her.

She was walking around the city when three of the governers came to her 'The President wants to see you, Mars.' Mars though perplexed at the request, followed them.

There stood the President, Palan Hase, with red hairand emerald eyes 'Mars, you – actually came.' He said in a apprehensive voice. 'So, well you're, uh- exiled, from I'Lexio.' He finally mustered up. Mars felt utterly confused. 'What? No not what, *why*?' 'Well Mars you remember about the political disagreements we've had with Nevada? Well we think you're causing it...'

She felt horrified. How could she do it? 'But why would I do that, Palan?...' One of the governers groaned at her calling Palan by his name casually. 'It's not *you*causing anything intentionally, it's the fact you're a dark pheonix, they carry curses with them so we suspect it's the curse that is bringing these misfortunes. So, you have to be exiled.. Sorry, Mars!'

Mars felt conflicted but before she could say anything more, one of the governers caught her hand and vanished in a poof of purple smoke Mars had been teleported out of I'Lexio to a shabby old cabin situated in the outskirts of Nevada. The governer vanished leaving no smoke behind leaving her all alone.

Mars sat down in front of the cabin, thinking about how embarassed Palan would be when the situation between Nevada and I'Lexio remains the same and they realised Mars wasn't causing any of it. But minues passed into hours and so did this thought, not a soul came to bring her back or to discuss the situation with her.

To give herself more hope Mars pretended that it might take a little longer for anything to happen. But as Mars waited as the sounds of bombs, guns explosions everything, that was happening around the border, slowly but steadily, turned quieter and quieter till the only sounds she could hear were people walking, talking, laughing and crying. She almost crumbled to the ground. She was the source of the problem. She caused it, she would never go to her lands. Ever. Again.

Mars turned to her cabin, slowly walking towards it. She decided to explore the cabin while she was still sane. She again went outside to see the cabin nicely, from the outside. To her shock she was met by ten's of hundred's of thousand's of dead and alive cockroaches. The cabin was clearly very old judging by the holes in the walls and roofs.

This was further proven as Mars went back in to the main room, it had a small television, which looked as if it was from 100 BC which Mars couldn't use as there was no electricity in the cabin. They didn't hate her, even though they exiled
her they didn't hate her.

That thought made her happy again and she went to the bedroom. One small, twin-sized bed with no mattress nor pillow and a poster was in there with a clock on the wall. She now accepted it, she was exiled.

A year passed, 2 years, 4 years but nothing changed in her cycle of nothingness, but 9 years in, a change had to be made. And a change was made.

She woke up to the red-hot sun once again and put on a jacket and jeans, she went outside to have a walk. She slowly got further and further till she saw a note reading out Mars Trailor, Cabin at the border. She suspiously opened the note.

Something is gonna happen tommorow.
My advice;

Get into Nevada and buy a couple litres of poultijuice.. you'll need it.. That's all I can say, Bye.

Nevada

Chapter Two

-Nevada-

Still suspious Mars went back to the cabin, ate a sandwhich she had bought from a local shop and went out once again. She started towards Nevada until she saw a glimpse of a street after which, she teleported. She went to one of the shops asking the shopkeeper 'Uh, do you have a Poultijuice.' He shook his head and Mars tried another shop asking the same thing, the shopkeeper replied negatively again.

She ran over to seven or eight more shops, then luckily on the ninth shop the woman standing in nodded and went out of sight then suddenly came back handing her a strange liquid in a giant bottle. She paid and teleported back to the cabin.

In an attempt to figure out what it did, she took a dead cockroach that was lying infront of her house and poured some of the Poultijuice on it. Then, out of the blue it started to move trying to get out of her hand, she dropped it and it fled.

Mars was shook, why did- well, the person who sent the note think I needed a- reviving juice- liquid thing? She walked back in and placed it on a table. Realizing the possibilities this juice brought. She hoped she wouldn't need to revive herself the next day.

She laid in her cabin doing nothing, as a soft knock reached her ears. She was startled to hear it but went to open the door. Outside stood two people. 'Who are you?' she asked quietly 'You don't remember me?' one replied in a sort of funny voice. 'Alex Ivan.' Memories flushed through Mars's head, 'and Hayden Jace.' 'well, why are you here?' she asked 'To take you back to I'Lexio.'

Sudden shock filled Mars's brain 'What? I'm coming- back' she asked peplexed 'Yeah, you are. But let me explain first, the Nevadian people started a bit of a political problem, which has become. Well, a really big issue. So we know you weren't like polluting their minds or something. Now let's go I might be fired if we go any later.' And with his words both of them vanished in poofs of orange smoke as Mars followed with her own poof of purple.

Voices, familiar and not, rang around Mars like angry bees. But another voice cut through, a voice that flashed memories more than ever. 'Mars!'

Colin Lark was her friend, her only friend he was slim and had medium blonde hair which covered half his face, with blue eyes and a grin on his face. He was also not a human, being a white dragon. They hadn't seen each other in nine whole years and there he was, standing The exact same as before.

Mars's expression changed almost automatically, from annoyed to ecstatic. Colin breathed, 'I thought they were lying- but you're back.'

'Wait so they told all of you but couldn't like I don't know write to me saying I can come back or something?' Colin started staring at Alex with a doesn't-she-know look. 'Uh, no-' Alex answered quietly. 'We were shocked you didn't try to escape by teleporting and hitting the border.' 'Border? I lived at the border and what don't I know?' Mars asked quickly.

'We had a magic border around the country so you wouldn't come back from exile, but you didn't try so we thought you found out, but either way you're amnesic so you could have forgotten-' Alex replied before 'I have amnesia?'

Exploring I'Lexio

Chapter Three

-Exploring I'Lexio-

Everyone started staring at her even more intensely and Colin answered first. '...You forgot you're amnesic? That's the first, well let's go I'm supposed to show you the capital since so much changed here.'

Mars hadn't had time to really look at Alex or Hayden yet. Alex had black hair not unlike hers and Hayden had chocolate brown hair which flew around with the wind. They both shared sapphire eyes that emanated their entire faces. Mars slowly walked away with Colin stillshocked about everything that had happened

Colin and Mars first went to the "Trailor Museum" 'This is probably the quickest way of catching you up on everything, because it was your family that even made it, you know, you probably don't, do you?' Colin said as they walked in the pearly white building. Mars saw more than she could've imagined, art, quotes, famous names and even sculptures. 'Remember? They made a Portrait of you, Alex, Palan and the new president, Evan Carl.' Mars's mind flashed 'There's a new president? What about Palan?' 'Chill!' He exclaimed. 'You're acting like Palan's dead! He's still in the capital, we still live in the apartment opposite to the "President's Palace".'

Those words calmed Mars way more than she'd think, 'Look at your Portrait, your artist was a load better at art than Alex and even Palan's artist.' He admitted in a slightly jealous voice. Her portrait was actually better than Mars thought it would be, she was floating with both her wings stretched out wearing a hoodie and leggings.

Next they went to the famous names.
Palan Hase, Previous president of I'Lexio, Evan Carl, Current president, Alex Ivan, Head of Security department. Then she saw none other than her name, *Mars Trailor, ex-Head of External Affairs department.*' Yeah, you were one of the best and youngest Politicians they've ever seen.' Colin said watching her staring at her name.

They then walked to the famous quotes, A secret is an unknown fact -Harvey Jace. 'Jace? Like Hayden Jace?' 'No that's his sister she also has a portrait over their. And yeah, you also have a quote- come to think about it, you, Alex Hayden and Harvey are all Nevadians yet your names are in everything the Trailor Muesum has, Famous names, portraits, quotes.

Mars turned to look at Harvey's portait, she was an exact replica of her brother, the same floaty brown hair and green eyes. Mars's eyes moved away from Harvey Jace.

'But then why was I exiled if I was- not to hurt you, Colin - But the greatest politician- ever?' She asked, Colin replied

'I-don't-know' quickly, too quickly. 'You know, don't you. You just don't want to tell me.' She said firmly. He stared for sometime then whispered 'You'll forget anyway, i'll just tell you, but' he glanced behind himself as though checking if anyone was there. 'Yeah I can say, just don't tell anyone, would you?'

Mars nodded and he started speaking 'President Evan, was one of the biggest reasons you got exiled. He hated dark pheonixes and I think you forgot but exiling you wasn't Palan's choice it was Evan's. But there is another reason that they didn't tell me, it was the decider of exiling you.' 'Oh, well I have another less serious question, where's your portrait or quote-' but before she could finish the question he burst out laughing saying. 'Mars i'm not one of the goverment officials! I'm a mechanical engineer, silly. We still have to see the News Wall, that's the main reason we came here, anyway.' And they went into the heart of the buiding once more, Mars saw a grey wall with a newspaper on it. 'The paper gets changed every week and a page is added every day *of*that week, here's a copy,'

Colin gave her a copy, and she started reading it, there were seven pages, one for each day in a week, Mars got to the last page quickly and saw a twelve year old boy smiling up at the camera, *Percy Ferin Yet To Be Found, Youngest shapeshifter in a century*still missing. 'What happened to this boy?' She asked looking at Colin, 'Well he went missing two months ago, but we know he's alive and safe, because he was found but he dissapeared again. Now, let's go back to my house, before either of us goes missing.' And with that they both vanished with a poof of purple and white smoke.

They both teleported to the middle of the capital, Colin took Mars's hand and in another poof of smoke vanished again this time to Colins living room. 'Oh, yeah-uh- sorry Mars but I don't have a guest bedroom' he said sadly. 'So? You have an amazingly beautiful couch I can sleep on.' Mars said easily.

'You're going to sleep on the couch?' he asked with a pleasantly suprised tone. 'Yeah, I slept on a cockroach-infested bed that didn't have a mattress that I kept falling off of it and hitting the hard floor back in exile, of yeah I didn't have a pillow I had a carboard plate.' she said. 'That. Is depressing' Colin said before teleporting to the bedroom. Mars layed on the couch looking outside the window and in seconds, fell fast asleep.

Spark

Chapter Four

-Spark-

With the reality of war setting in, I'Lexio began preparations, for what they called The CC war naming it after the president of Nevada, Charles Clayton. Mars, using some magic did them a huge favor by making a barrrier around I'Lexio so no Nevadian – except her, Alex, Hayden or Harvey– could enter.

Mars woke up the next morning to a loud ring of bells, 'Oh, Colin! Shut the bells up' she yelled covering her ears. 'Well, wake up. Its 11 for heaven's sake.' He replied as Mars teleported off the couch and in a jiffy was standing right infront of him wearing her usual hoodie. 'Yeah, so let's leave. Evan might aswell kill me or worse, pour water on me.' Mars said quickly before vanishing once again so quickly the poof was almost not visible anymore.

Mars hated water more than anything she had gotten hives atleast 50 times back in exile because of it. She had Aquagenic Urticaria, allergy to water.

As the town hall came to focus it all looked fine, but one blink later it was on fire. Mars, in shock looked behind her to see the rest of the politicans staring at the blazing building. Slowly firefighters came and extingushed the flames as Mars backed away from the fire and more importanly water.

But there was clearly fire still inside the building no one seemed to want to enter. She didn't know why but she wanted to go inside, she walked in slowly making sure not to touch any water. Everyone was staring at her she walked right into fire and it burned out with abnormal purple smoke.

Confused as she was, she did it for every spark she saw. And was far into the building when she saw a book on a table. Doubtfully, she decided to take the book. And read the top of it, diary, DON'T READ. Mars' confusion didn't end there as the name written on it was Evan Carl. This was his diary. Mars quickly teleported it back to Colin's house and continued burning out the fire till it was completely gone.

She teleported outside and saw the hall perfectly fine and her feeling like she was on fire. She either absorbed or (most probably) walked on so much fire she felt she was ablaze. She walked back to Colin ignoring the others staring at her. To her annoyance he too was staring at her.

The day went by as if it was 360 degree flip, starting with fire and ending with rain and a lot of smog. Mars stayed inside Colin's house examining the diary she found in the town hall. It was for a fact Evan's but 20 year old Evan's. Apparently the diary was Evan's when he was 20 which was ten years ago.

Mars decided to see what was in the diary but before she could read the first page. The window she was sitting next to, flew open and rain drenched her, almost howling in pain Mars threw the book to a table and teleported to a towel painfully drying herself.

The book however was not even slightly wet and Colin was still asleep, the window slowly shut itself - this time tighter -. Mars wanted to open the book but this time away from the window.

So she took the book and opened it near another window and this one also opened taking long enough for Mars to run and close the window with magic. "This book is cursed." She thought to herself putting the book down once again and planned to try again tomorrow night and went to her couch to sleep.

The next morning was different when Colin and Mars came to the town hall expecting a regular day, they got the complete opposite.
'Alright everyone we're starting a new type of training, at first we just did physical's now we're using magic. So if you would come over here and tell -and show if you can- your ability.' It was Palan, standing infront of the chairs they were all sitting in.

One by one they walked up except Mars. She stayed on her chair till everyone had gone except her. She depressingly walked over and painstakingly said. 'I can -well- absorb fire, and well I have wings and- uh -telekinesis. Like this.' She lifted her vacant chair and everyone started staring at it. 'For the fire, you saw me doing it yesterday and- uh. And, yeah that's it.' She went back to her chair and sat through the rest of the class until the lecture ended.

The Dream

Chapter Five

-The Dream-

'Mars and Alex, would you come here.' Mars and Alex teleported to the front again. 'So as you both know you're the only Nevadians here meaning your magic is alot more useful because you both were taught by Nevadians you'll know alot of their tricks, so would you like to tell us some tips. Mars, you can go first.'

'Well, I haven't seen my family in a decade but I remember one thing my mom taught me, when someone is using offense on you. Use defense, this will get their guard up for secret attacks that makes them predictable and because of that, defeatable.' She said attacking her head trying to remember another one. 'And I don't remember another one.'

Alex walked a little more forward and started. 'I don't really have any tips, just, well watch- your back, I guess.'

They both teleported outside. Mars waited for Colin as Alex teleported again. Colin came after five minutes of waiting, 'Sorry, Palan wanted a word.' and with that they went back.

Mars spent the evening reading up on dark pheonix magic and how to open mysterious magical diaries. The evening flew away in what felt like minutes and before she knew it she was eating dinner with Colin. Tonight she had followed an outdated recipe for noodles and flat bread with cottage cheese filling. Which Colin insisted tasted alot better than her usual junk

Soon she was sitting on the couch after a suprisingly good dinner, ready to sleep. Mars laid down and after a long staring contest with the ceiling, fell asleep. Mars woke up not in her couch but in a room with Harvey.

'Why did I even trust you, a person who managed to get exiled at age sixteen?' She vanished and her brother took her place. 'Bringing you back from exile was my biggest mistake, forget I brought you back, would you?' He too vanished Mars's confusion started to fuse with disbelief and slight hurt.

Suddenly a little boy appeard and vanished in a second. Mars was back in her couch now wide awake and still looking at the ceiling, she didn't remember anything. 'Well I' (yawn) 'guess I can try to figure out how that diary works.' She took the diary from the table.

Mars sat again staring at the diary (this time far away from a window). Opening it once again.. This time the book shut close instantly she tried again with no difference. Mars even tried to open it sitting on the floor keeping the book on the table still it wouldn't budge.

Mars wanted to ask Colin to try and open it. But knowing Colin would without doubt tell Evan, she decided on keeping her mouth shut. Soon she was out ofIdeas, but she had one thought roaming her brain like a train. What if she opened it with magic. It was worth a shot.

She put the tightly shut book back on the table and tried one last time to open it normally making no difference. Turned back to her original idea. Slowly the book started to open but shut tightly again. Se tried one more time even more carefully and after 5 minutes of patiently waiting, it was opened.

Pages

Chapter Six

-Pages-

Mars started to scroll through the index hoping to find something interesting when she found Mortal Pheonix plan, Doomsday. Confused, Mars went to that page number and started reading.

Dear Diary,
1990, SEPTEMBER 11
Today is the day I finally executed the Mortal Pheonix Scheme, after months of work. (a quick reminder of the plan in case I forget.)
1.Go to the White Festival
2.Make "THE Epic" speech
3.Burn everything to ashes

These words grabbed Mars's attention alot, the"White Festival" rang bells in her head. Mars had been to the White Festival when she was still in Nevada. Mars decided to continue reading and find out more.

"Hello, everyone. I am Evan Carl I've hosted this brilliant event for you. You will never forget this event or these words, I thought you

would've learned not to trust me. Let. The. Show. Begin..." With these words I lit the stage and ran for it making sure the trail of gasoline was alight. The entire place would've burnt in minutes.

Mars was losing it, Mortal Pheonix Plan? More like Dark Pheonix Extinction plan. She would've done anything else but she had to keep reading, even if she'll forget this information was still important.

To my suprise unlike the plan stated there was still one single Dark pheonix alive. I had realized this as I saw the festival burn to the ground. On a hill near the burning building stood a teenage girl staring at the flames which (probably) murdered her family-

Then suddenly everything made sense as though the missing piece of the jigsaw was slotted in. She was the teenage girl, the reason she was an orphan was Evan.

Note

Chapter Seven

-Note-

With the war ever closer physical and magical sessions turned into more of a military training than any of them expected. Mars's guard was always up and when she wasn't training (theory or practical) she was searching for anything that would help her, like a dog digging up a bone.

She walked in the building where they kept magic lessons. To her suprise there were only ten or so, other people. She sat next to Colin and asked him 'Hey, Colin where's everyone?' 'Today's class was optional, because a lot of us know the spells we're learning today already.' He answered. 'But it would be useful to attend this class.

Slowly the room started getting a little more full but then Palan arrived meaning that no else would be coming. 'Today, is an interesting lesson. Killing curses.' This was not what Mars expected.

'there are two curses, Hatya and Everin. Hatya can kill in under ten seconds, Everin can kill someone in a minute. I wouldn't want to show you how they look but I can tell you how it feels, Hatya makes your vision blurry, its actually pretty painless it might feel a bit itchy but otherwise painless. Everin makes it so your body doesn't take in oxygen, so unless your an amazing breath-holder you'll die under a minute or atleast a couple minutes.'

As the training session ended thirty minutes later, Mars was about to teleport to the library like she always did when 'Mars, where on earth do you keep vanishing of to after training?' It was Palan, he clearly knew Mars was teleporting off after training with Colin but for a week she'd been teleporting without him.

Mars was starting to feel as though the war had started even though it hadn't. She had woken up from the same nightmare for what seemed the hundredth time. And as soon as she got ready and walked out of Colin's house with him saw a note, curious, they decided to go to the town hall before opening it.

As they reached, Colin explained to Evan about the note and as Mars was waiting she decided to sneak a peak. She started reading the note

I'Lexio, It is me Charles Clayton here to inform you that some of you might get fried on friday. In other words the war we've all been waiting for is due next Friday.
Yours truly,
-Charles Clayton

Mars was extremely confused by the time she finished reading the note. By now Evan, Colin, Palan and some other politicians had came and Mars started reading to them the dreadful letter.

'Mars, this could easily be a ploy, you know. If we're all ready for war and are waiting at the border where the two nations meet they could just go to the ocean side of I'Lexio and swim in with a boat and start attacking-'

'Evan, if they did that it would be war.' Palan cut him off. Palan had always been the one who acknowledged reality with open arms and it always made Mars feel as if she was eighteen again the youngest politician this world has ever seen. Palan was still president and she never knew about her fate. Just a kid in an adult's world.

With the letter in everyone's thought process, training and session time increased, people were practising and searching stuff up more than ever, soon everyone would be ready for the war.

Mars had started getting bored as there was nothing she could do. Unlike everyone Mars knew perfectly well how to use her abilities. So she bid her time till the war had to come.

*

It was thursday night. Mars had made (with a lot of help from Colin) a strange chessy dish called Lasagne. Stomachs content, they went to bed.

It was almost midnight when a loud BOOM! woke Mars, she ran outside to see a word in glowing scarlet plastered on to the sky "The". Another loud BOOM! Mars' hands flew to shield her ears another word this time in glowing lavender "War" yet another BOOM! Made Mars fall to the ground, this time two words in vibrant green. "Has begun". In one last BOOM all the turned white and faded into cloud.

She looked around her to see thousands of people in their night-suits staring at exactly where the words were. The message slowly sinking in. Too, slowly.

Poofs of different colours filled her vision as in a second, people started disappearing and re-appearing in flashes of light till everyone from politicians to the military came. The war had truly begun. Mars (who had slept fully-clothed) instantly teleported to the border with everyone else.

Duels were happening left, right and center, people losing their lives, children getting orphaned just like her. The sheer wastage this war was causing staggered Mars.

At that moment, Mars remembered that she is special, she is a phoenix.. a dark phoenix.. the only dark phoenix living. While people blamed for causing chaos and discord, she realized that the pheonix in her is pushing to bring an end to this war, not to people's lives. With this thought, a strong force seemed to flow through her veins and burst out of her body. A blinding purple light emanating from her covered the whole region bringing all the fighters to a standstill.

Mars's voice boomed outloud, commanding both Nevadians and i'Lexians to stop this war immediately. '*Stop at once! You've all blamed dark pheonixes for years.. saying that we caused wars, chaos and pain! And here you are! Causing nothing, but more people like me to lose their lives, parents and family! I was born in Nevada, lived most of my life in i'Lexio and even more in exile. I have realized that love for one's own country is all well and good, but not to the extent of cruelty against other countries. Today, I declare myself a free phoenix, I do not belong to either of the countries, but I would use my powers for both in a constructive manner. Anyone who causes discord, enmity and war will have to answer to me...*'

Everyone looked a little bit guilty and completely awestruck by the purple glow and the words coming from Mars. The utter truth of the words struck a chord in everyone's heart. People slowly started leaving the war zone taking their injured friends and family with them.

We can all expect a peaceful future for both countries, thanks to the only dark pheonix alive..... Mars Trailer..

www.ingramcontent.com/pod-product-compliance
Lightning Source LLC
Chambersburg PA
CBHW021408160726
47994CB00007B/3131